Hey Diddle Diddle

and

Hey Diddle Doodle

Retold by Brian Moses
Illustrated by Jill Newton

Crabtree Publishing Company

www.crabtreebooks.com

Crabtree Publishing Company
www.crabtreebooks.com
1-800-387-7650

PMB 59051, 350 Fifth Ave.
59th Floor,
New York, NY 10118

616 Welland Ave.
St. Catharines, ON
L2M 5V6

Published by Crabtree Publishing in 2012

Series editor: Jackie Hamley
Editor: Kathy Middleton

Proofreader: Reagan Miller
Series advisor: Dr. Hilary Minns
Series designer: Peter Scoulding
Production coordinator and
  Prepress technician: Margaret Amy Salter
Print coordinator: Katherine Berti

Text (Hey Diddle Doodle)
© Brian Moses 2008
Illustration © Jill Newton 2008

The rights of Brian Moses
to be identified as the author
of Hey Diddle Doodle and
Jill Newton as the illustrator of
this Work have been asserted.

First published in 2008
by Franklin Watts
(A division of Hachette
Children's Books)

Printed in Canada/102018/
MA20180913

Library and Archives Canada
Cataloguing in Publication

Moses, Brian, 1950-
    Hey diddle diddle, and Hey diddle doodle /
retold by Brian Moses ; illustrated by Jill Newton.

(Tadpoles: nursery rhymes)
Issued also in electronic format.
ISBN 978-0-7787-7884-4 (bound).--
ISBN 978-0-7787-7896-7 (pbk.)

    1. Nursery rhymes, English. I. Newton, Jill,
1964- II. Title. III. Series: Tadpoles (St. Catharines,
Ont.). Nursery rhymes

PZ8.3.M67He 2012   j398.8   C2012-902469-4

Library of Congress
Cataloging-in-Publication Data

Moses, Brian, 1950-
  Hey diddle diddle and Hey diddle doodle /
retold by Brian Moses ; illustrated by Jill Newton.
    p. cm. -- (Tadpoles: nursery rhymes)
  ISBN 978-0-7787-7884-4 (reinforced library
binding : alk. paper) -- ISBN 978-0-7787-7896-7
(pbk. : alk. paper) -- ISBN 978-1-4271-7923-4
(electronic pdf : alk. paper) -- ISBN 978-1-4271-
8038-4 (electronic html : alk. paper)
  1. Nursery rhymes. 2. Children's poetry. [1.
Nursery rhymes.] I. Newton, Jill, 1964- ill. II. Title.
III. Title: Hey diddle diddle. IV. Title: Hey diddle
doodle.
    PZ8.3.M8435Hey 2012
  398.8--dc23
                                                    2012015486

Hey Diddle Diddle

Jill Newton

"I live by the
sea in Somerset with
my dog, Bob, and my
horse, Spinney. I spend
my time running, riding,
and drawing."

Hey diddle diddle,
the cat and the fiddle,

The cow jumped over the moon.

The little dog laughed
to see such fun,

And the dish ran away
with the spoon!

Hey Diddle Diddle

Hey diddle diddle,

the cat and the fiddle,

The cow jumped over the moon.

The little dog laughed

to see such fun,

And the dish ran away

with the spoon!

Can you point to the
rhyming words?

Hey Diddle Doodle

Brian Moses

"I have a golden labrador called Honey who spends a lot of her time trying to get through the garden fence to visit the poodle next door."

Hey diddle doodle,
the pipe and the poodle,

The frog hopped over the star.

The big tiger roared to
see such tricks,

And the fork zoomed
away in his car!

Hey Diddle Doodle

Hey diddle doodle,

the pipe and the poodle,

The frog hopped over the star.

The big tiger roared

to see such tricks,

And the fork zoomed

away in his car!

Can you point to the
rhyming words?

Puzzle Time!

How many cats and dogs can you see in this picture?

Notes for adults

TADPOLES NURSERY RHYMES are structured for emergent readers. The books may also be used for read-alouds or shared reading with young children.

The language of nursery rhymes is often already familiar to an emergent reader. Seeing the rhymes in print helps build phonemic awareness skills. The alternative rhymes extend and enhance the reading experience further, and encourage children to be creative with language and make up their own rhymes.

IF YOU ARE READING THIS BOOK WITH A CHILD, HERE ARE A FEW SUGGESTIONS:

1. Make reading fun! Choose a time to read when you and the child are relaxed and have time to share the story.

2. Recite the nursery rhyme together before you start reading. What might the alternative rhyme be about? Brainstorm ideas.

3. Encourage the child to reread the rhyme and to retell it using his or her own words. Invite the child to use the illustrations as a guide.

4. Help the child identify the rhyming words when the whole rhymes are repeated on pages 12 and 22. This activity builds phonological awareness and decoding skills. Encourage the child to make up alternative rhymes.

5. Give praise! Children learn best in a positive environment.

IF YOU ENJOYED THIS BOOK, WHY NOT TRY ANOTHER TITLE FROM TADPOLES: NURSERY RHYMES?

Baa, Baa, Black Sheep and Baa, Baa, Pink Sheep	978-0-7787-7883-7 RLB	978-0-7787-7895-0 PB
Humpty Dumpty and Humpty Dumpty at Sea	978-0-7787-7885-1 RLB	978-0-7787-7897-4 PB
Itsy Bitsy Spider and Itsy Bitsy Beetle	978-0-7787-7886-8 RLB	978-0-7787-7898-1 PB

VISIT WWW.CRABTREEBOOKS.COM FOR OTHER CRABTREE BOOKS.

Answers

There are four dogs and six cats.